TITCH
AND
DAISY

Pat Hutchins

TITCH AND

Julia MacRae Books **JM**

LONDON SYDNEY AUCKLAND JOHANNESBURG

DAISY

3 5 7 9 10 8 6 4 2

Copyright © 1996 Pat Hutchins

Pat Hutchins has asserted her right under
the Copyright, Designs and Patents Act, 1988
to be identified as the author of this work

First published in the USA in 1996 by
Greenwillow Books

First published in the United Kingdom in 1996 by
Julia MacRae
Random House, 20 Vauxhall Bridge Road, London SW1V 2SA

Random House Australia (Pty) Limited
20 Alfred Street, Milsons Point, Sydney,
New South Wales 2061, Australia

Random House New Zealand Limited
18 Poland Road, Glenfield,
Auckland 10, New Zealand

Random House South Africa (Pty) Limited
PO Box 337, Bergvlei 2012, South Africa

Random House UK Limited Reg. No. 954009

A CIP catalogue record for this book is
available from the British Library

ISBN 1-85681-621-4

Printed in China

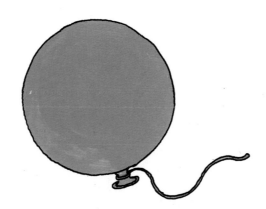

For Barbara and Henning
to read to their grandchildren

Titch didn't want to go to the party. "You'll make new friends," said Mother, "and Daisy will be there."

He hid behind the door and
watched them playing all his
favourite games.
He wished Daisy were there.

Titch looked for Daisy, but
Daisy wasn't there.
"Hello," said the other children.
"Come and play with us!"
But Titch didn't want to play
if Daisy wasn't there.

"Come and dance with us!"
said the other children.
But Titch didn't want to dance
if Daisy wasn't there.

So he crept behind the sofa
and watched them dancing
all his favourite dances.
He wished Daisy were there.

"Come and sing with us!" said
the other children.
But Titch didn't want to sing
if Daisy wasn't there.

So he peeped out of the
cupboard and listened to them
singing all his favourite songs.
He wished Daisy were there.

"Come and eat with us!" said
the other children.
But Titch didn't want to eat
if Daisy wasn't there.

He crawled under the table,
which was covered with all his
favourite things to eat.
He wished Daisy were there.

And she was.

"I hid under the table when I couldn't find you," said Daisy. "I kept wishing you were here."

"PLEASE come and eat with us,"
said the other children.
And Titch and Daisy did.

They ate all their favourite food.

And they danced,
and sang
all their favourite songs,

and played all their favourite games,

and made lots of new friends.